To Ann Marie,

without whose wholehearted and energetic participation

this latest edition of the first sequel to *Caps for Sale*

(as well as its musical cassette version) would never have materialized.

—E.S.

Originally published as *Pezzo the Peddler and the Circus Elephant*
by Abelard-Schuman, 1967

Circus Caps for Sale
Copyright © 1967, 2002 by Esphyr Slobodkina
Manufactured in China by South China Printing Company Ltd.
All rights reserved.
www.harperchildrens.com

Library of Congress Cataloging-in-Publication Data
Slobodkina, Esphyr, date.
[Caps for sale]
Circus caps for sale / story and pictures by Esphyr Slobodkina.—1st ed.
p. cm.
Summary: A peddler who sells caps by balancing them all on his head is invited to
do an act in the circus.
ISBN 0-06-029655-0 — ISBN 0-06-029656-9 (lib. bdg.)
ISBN 0-06-443793-0 (pbk.)
[1. Hats—Fiction. 2. Peddlers and peddling—Fiction. 3. Circus—Fiction.]
I. Title.
PZ7.S6334 Ci 2002   2001024966
[E]—dc21   CIP
                                                                    AC

Typography by Al Cetta
❖

CIRCUS
CAPS
FOR SALE

Story and Pictures by
Esphyr Slobodkina

HARPERCOLLINSPUBLISHERS

Early one morning,
Pezzo the peddler woke up.
He jumped out of bed
and began to dress.

First he put on his socks.
Next he put on his clean white shirt.
Then he put on his fine
black-and-white checked trousers.
And last he put on his
fancy yellow shoes.

Then the peddler put on his jacket
and his lucky cap, picked up his
wares, and was ready to go to work.

The peddler walked fast—
as fast as he could without upsetting his caps.
For, you see, the peddler sold caps.
Only instead of carrying the caps in a bundle
on his back,
he carried them on top of his head.

First he had on his own
black-and-white checked cap,
then a bunch of gray caps,
then a bunch of brown caps,
then a bunch of blue caps,
and, on the very top,
a bunch of red caps.

As soon as he got to town,

he began to call out,

"Caps! Caps for sale! Fifty cents a cap!"

But the street was strangely quiet.

No man stopped the peddler to try on a cap.

No woman leaned out of a window

to see if they were really good caps.

No children ran after the peddler.

There weren't even any dogs to follow him.

But as he came nearer to the town square, the peddler
began to hear the sounds of voices and loud music.

"Of course," he thought, "it must be the county fair."

Sure enough, the nearer
he got, the clearer he saw that it
was indeed a county fair.

The Ferris wheel turned.
The merry-go-round went
round and round.
And at the far end
of the square, the peddler saw
an enormous circus tent.

"Caps for sale!
Caps for sale!"
The peddler began to call.
But before he got to saying,
"Fifty cents a cap!"

B-O-O-M!
went a big drum
as the circus parade came
around the corner.

"Oh, well," sighed the peddler.
"He is bigger than I.
I'll wait until he goes by."

Next a great big
bass horn came into view,
and began to thump.

OOM-PA-PA! OOM-PA-PA!
OOM-PAPA-PA!

"Oh, well," sighed the peddler
again, "he is louder than I.
I can wait until he goes by."

But what came around the corner next
was not just a big drum or a loud bass horn
but the whole circus band!

The trumpets shrilled,
the trombones blared,
and the little piccolos went *tweedle-dee-dee!*

The big cymbals went *B-O-N-G!* and
the tiny triangle went *P-I-N-G!*

"Oh, well," sighed the peddler for the third time.
"There are so many of them!
I'll just have to wait until they go by."

The peddler saw the circus riders
prance by on their plumed white horses.

He saw the fierce lions and tigers, and
the chattering monkeys in their cages.

He saw a truckload of trained seals
and dancing dogs go by.

Four striped zebras,
three long-necked giraffes,

two double-humped camels,
and one huge elephant.

It was a wonderful parade.
Even the peddler thought so . . .
until he met up with Jumbo.

Jumbo was the circus elephant
in the parade.
He liked to perform tricks
to amuse the crowd.

Sometimes he would simply take
some peanuts from a child's hand
and put them in his mouth.
Sometimes he would fill his trunk
with water and pretend
to give himself a shower.
And sometimes he would steal
a hat from a man in the crowd,
try it on his rider's head,
and return it to the stranger.

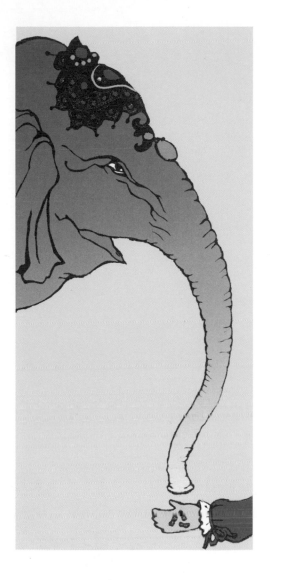

Naturally, when Jumbo saw the peddler
with his pile of caps, he reached
for it with his long trunk.

In a second, there was a
very surprised elephant,
a very amused crowd,
and a very, very sad peddler.
For all the red caps,
blue caps,
brown caps,
and gray caps
came flying down
in every direction.

When the tumblers, the jugglers, and the clowns
saw all the caps falling, they thought it was a
new trick the big boss added to the parade.
So, they each caught a cap and went on with their acts:

The clowns clowned in brown caps.
The tumblers tumbled in gray caps.
And the jugglers did their juggling
with the red and blue caps.

The crowd roared with laughter.

Everybody was delighted—except the peddler.

Down the main street and all around the town,

the parade marched, with the peddler running after it,

calling, "My caps! My caps!

Please give me back my caps!"

But nobody paid any attention to him.

Nobody even heard his voice.

At last, the peddler gave up.
He sat down on a bench
under a big tree and
watched the parade
disappear around the corner.

When the parade was over,
the circus people gathered in the
big top to congratulate the
big boss on his clever new trick.

"Thank you! Thank you,
my friends,"
said the big boss, "but I had
nothing to do with it."

"Then who did?"
asked the jugglers.
"Who did?"
asked the tumblers.
"Who did?"
asked the clowns.
"Jumbo did," said Joe,
the elephant rider.

And he told the circus people about the little peddler.

Joe also tried to show how the peddler carried all his caps. But when he got to the first brown cap, all the caps fell down.

Then one of the clowns tried to put
on the caps, but when he got to the
first blue cap, all the caps fell down.

Everybody tried.

Even one of the jugglers tried,
but when he got to the last red cap,
all the caps fell down.

"Aha!" said the big boss. "Perhaps it is
not such an easy trick, after all!
And if it is not such an easy
trick to do, my friends, does it not
belong in the circus?"

"Yes, yes!" shouted all the circus people.
So, the big boss sent two tall men to find
the little peddler.

The peddler
was not at all hard to find,
for he was still sitting
on the bench under the tree,
thinking his sad thoughts.

"Come quickly!" said the two
tall men.
"The big boss himself wants to
talk to you."

So the peddler went.

"Hello, there!" said the big boss to the peddler.
"They tell me you can carry all these caps on
your head without ever dropping a single one.
Neat trick, I say, if you can do it!"

"Yes, sir, I can," said the peddler.

He knelt in front of the caps.
First he put the bunch of brown caps
on top of the bunch of gray caps.
Then he put the bunch of
blue caps on top of the bunch
of brown caps
Then, on the very top,
he put the bunch
of red caps.

Very carefully, he picked up the whole pile
and put it on top of his own
black-and-white checked cap.

Then slowly, *very* slowly, he got up from his
knees and began to walk around, calling out,
"Caps for sale! Caps for sale!
Fifty cents a cap!"

"Bravo! Bravo!" shouted the big boss.

"Bravo, bravo, bravo!" shouted the rest
of the circus people.

"How would you like to do your act in
the circus ring?" asked the big boss.

"I-I don't know," stammered Pezzo.
"I am only a peddler who sells caps.
But if you really want me to . . ."

"Of course we do," said the big boss.
"There's nobody else like you."

That evening, when the circus lights went on,
the show was really grand.

There were horse riders
and elephant drivers.

There were trained lions and tamed tigers.

There were dancing dogs and talking seals.

There were tightrope walkers
and jugglers,

and tumblers,

and clowns.

And, of course, there was the peddler.

Everyone did their acts very well.

But most of all, people liked the peddler.
They clapped and whistled
when they saw how he carried
(on top of his own black-and-white checked cap)
the gray caps,
the brown caps,
the blue caps,
and, on the very top, the red caps,
without dropping a single one.

The peddler was delighted.
He walked around the
ring, feeling very straight
and tall, and calling, "Caps for sale!
Caps for sale!
Fifty cents a cap!"

After the show, Pezzo the peddler sold
all his gray, brown, blue, and red caps.
Someone even wanted to buy his own
black-and-white checked cap.

But the peddler wouldn't part with it—
it was his lucky cap, he said. And, besides,
it matched his own black-and-white
checked trousers.

THE END